For children and adolescents to help navigate the emotional current of the world.

The Invisible Riptide is a story of hope, healing, and connection. It is a tool for all ages and has life lessons meant for all. The illustrations are as powerful as the words, leaving room for the subconscious to show us a way towards achieving real health and balance. The core of true happiness — deep connection and feeling.

"They have a name for every color there is ... except "Lonely."
– WOODY DURWOOD

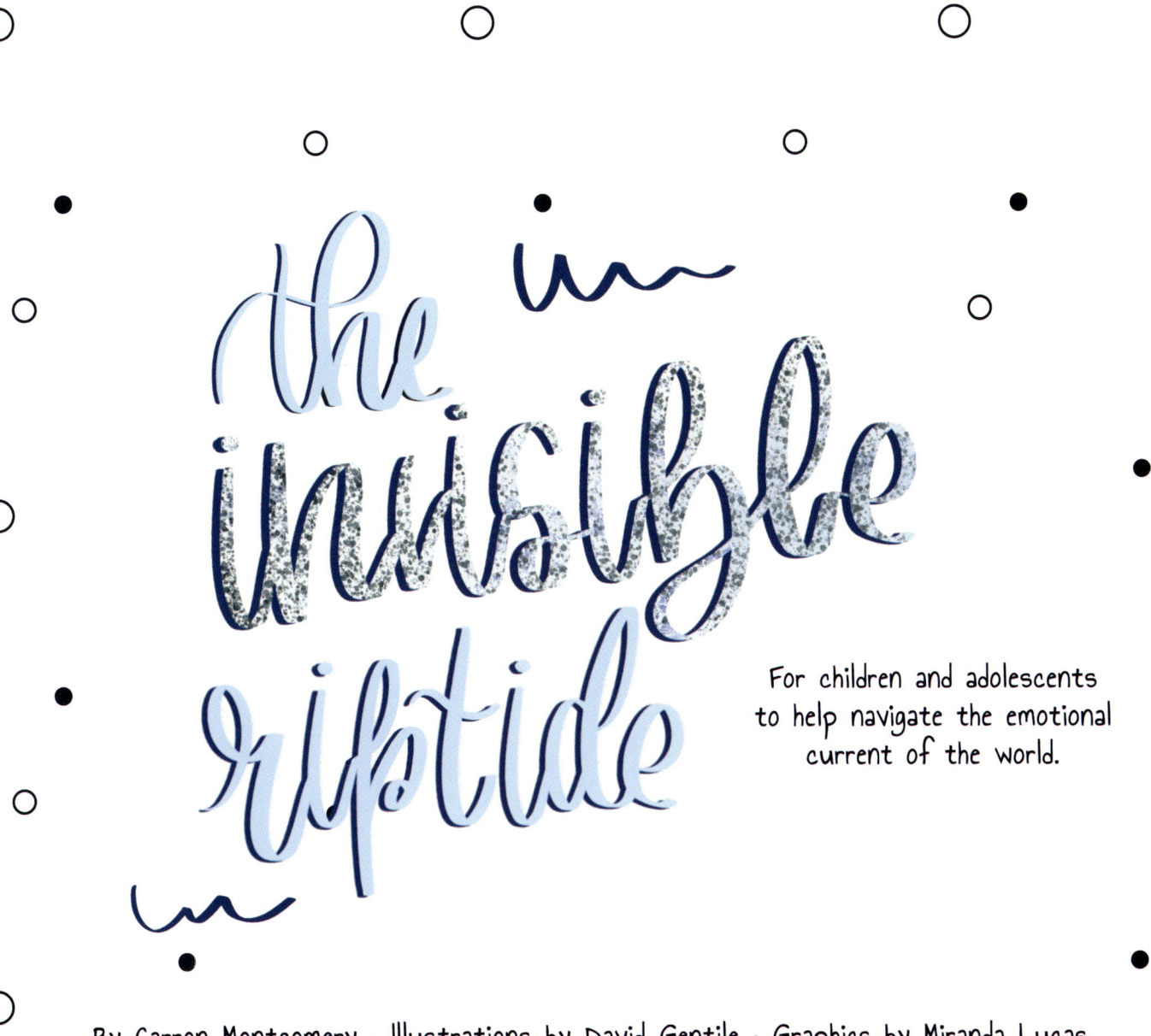

the invisible riptide

For children and adolescents to help navigate the emotional current of the world.

By Carron Montgomery · Illustrations by David Gentile · Graphics by Miranda Lucas

© 2021 The Invisible Riptide
Donnelly-Kilroy Publications

Dedicated to my incredible clients, who have courageously shown me what being a kid looks and feels like during a pandemic. To my husband, who patiently watched me work long hours and never stopped believing in me. To my spunky daughter, for showing me how to persevere in every way, and to my sons, who gave me countless snuggles.

A special thanks to my mother and father for teaching me the value of REAL life lessons; ones meant to be carried from one generation to the next.

And lastly, thank you to my mentor and therapist, Dr. Eric Kulick. You have helped me in more ways than words can express. Let's normalize that even therapists need therapy!

the invisible riptide

Stella woke up one day and felt a funny feeling in her belly. She wondered, "What could this be?"

Stella raced down the stairs to tell her mother.
She ran so quickly that she stumbled over the dog!

Her mother frantically asked, "What in the world is going on?"

Stella was out of breath as she said, "I woke up with a swirling, whirling feeling in my belly and head!"

Her mother quickly said, "Oh, Stella, I'm sure you are just fine. Maybe your belly just needs food? Or maybe you ate something funny last night."

Stella knew that wasn't right, but she didn't argue with her mother.

Stella knew what an empty belly felt like, and this was not it! Her tummy wasn't growling or puffy. It was swirling and whirling with all sorts of feelings: sadness, worry, loneliness, anxiety, and confusion.

It felt like her own invisible riptide — SCARY and out of control.

Stella started to wonder if she was all alone. She was confused and thought, "How could this be?"

When Stella saw her friends, she asked if they had a swirling and whirling feeling in their tummies and heads too. She was shocked when they all said, "YES!" Stella could hardly believe she wasn't alone! "Other people felt this way too!" She hadn't imagined it after all.

Not only did her friends feel the same feelings as Stella, but they had also tried explaining them to their parents. Sadly, they all got the same response that Stella had. Even their teacher thought the kids may be hungry or tired. The children began to wonder, "How could this be? How could all the adults around them not feel all of the swirling and whirling in their tummies and heads – the invisible riptides?"

"This is too much," Stella declared, "We are just kids and I will not let us down. I will continue to demand answers until they explain why all of us feel this way! The swirling and whirling around in our bellies must come to an end!"

Stella was PERSISTENT. She never backed down. Finally, her mother decided that she was out of ideas and didn't know what else to do. So she thought that they could go to a therapist and both learn to understand the invisible riptide that was taking hold of Stella. Her mom explained that a therapist is like a feelings doctor who knows all about the invisible riptide.

Stella felt a little nervous, since she had never seen a therapist before, but she was excited to have her voice heard.

The next day, Stella went to see Ms. Tina, her therapist. Ms. Tina was eager to learn all about Stella and her feelings. Stella smiled as she thought to herself, "I have come to the right place."

Stella told Ms. Tina all about her invisible riptide and all the swirling and whirling going on in her belly and head. She explained to Ms. Tina that sometimes these feelings would come and go, and sometimes they got so BIG that it felt like she was drowning underwater and all alone.

Ms. Tina explained to Stella that when our bellies and heads are swirling and whirling, it's our jumbled up feelings and thoughts trying to come out. She had Stella's attention now!

Ms. Tina asked if Stella could remember when she first noticed the swirling and whirling invisible riptide. Stella paused and started to search her brain. Finally, the answer came. Stella realized that her invisible riptide had shown up when something called the coronavirus entered the world. She was confused, because she felt happy and lucky to feel so safe in her home with her family, playing games, cooking and watching her favorite shows. Ms. Tina helped Stella understand that physical and emotional safety are different, but equally important. "Emotional safety?" Stella thought, "What's that?"

Her invisible riptide had gotten so big because she had **never, ever, ever** had this much time alone in her head before and she'd never had so many changes and uncertainty in her ENTIRE life! Suddenly she realized her friends and parents hadn't either.

Ms. Tina explained to Stella that the invisible riptide was actually her body's way of trying to make sense of the world and was like Stella's very own emotional thermometer. Her feelings were there to give her important information to help her make sense of the world and guide her towards physical and emotional safety.

Ms. Tina taught Stella that emotional safety means feeling safe to share her feelings and having her boundaries respected by the people around her. And most importantly that all feelings are ok!

Ms. Tina also explained that when we don't have healthy outlets and activities, we can get stuck in our head and it can feel like you are swimming in a swirling, whirling sea.

Ms. Tina explained that the riptide was so powerful that others could feel it too. She called it the emotional current of the world. Stella learned that her brain could feel the riptide of all of those around her. Finally things started to make sense. No wonder Stella's mom had been so cranky and her dad was on edge all of the time. Stella was certain that they too must have an invisible riptide.

Stella and Ms. Tina worked hard to understand this massive invisible riptide controlling the world. They worked together and discovered what fed the riptide, the things that made it bigger, and what helped the riptide's current slow down and find peace.

Of all the tools Stella learned, she was most excited to share that dancing and exercise could help. Stella loved nothing more than dancing in the wind like no one was watching. Dancing carefree in the moment, just letting herself be.

Stella also learned that her invisible riptide had gotten so big because she hadn't been able to connect with other people when she was home. Stella realized that being alone and isolated made her feel yucky and confused. She was so excited that she taught her friends and family the importance of feeling connected to one another. Stella loudly began to chant, "People need people! People need people!"

Stella made a new
declaration — It's time
to ask for help and to
talk about your feelings! Most
importantly, it's okay NOT to be okay.
It doesn't mean something bad will happen, it
simply means something needs to change.

Stella taught her world something special. Feeling anxious, worried, sad, mad, or confused are all okay. Those feelings are part of what makes us human! She also taught people to ask for help and to lean on each other. After that day, all of the adults around her started to share their feelings and thoughts, too! Mental health became more important and people started to feel more free. They were no longer embarrassed of their feelings or of needing help.

They learned that together, they could do anything!

About the Author
Carron Montgomery, MSCP, LPC, RPT

Carron Montgomery started a private practice nine years ago with two other women. Their practice specializes in treating anxiety, depression, OCD, trauma, grief and loss. Carron is a Licensed Professional Counselor, Registered Play Therapist and Level II trained in EMDR. She utilizes a client-centered approach that includes the importance of collaborating with each client's team of professionals and primary caregivers. At the beginning of her career, she worked for two nonprofits; the first specializing in sexual abuse and the second working with low-income families and trauma. She currently treats ages 4 and up and often utilizes family therapy and parental support sessions.

She is also a presenter for churches, schools and various organizations. At the beginning of the pandemic she saw a huge need that was not being addressed. This book was written to start the conversations in the community, and provide a much needed resource to be used by schools, community organizations and families. Discussion questions, activities and other supporting materials can be found at www.theinvisibleriptide.com

About the Illustrator
David Gentile

David Gentile is a beautiful artist and soul. He retired and found his love of drawing while he was the president of BCBSKC. A coworker entered him in a drawing contest and his hobby turned into a passion. After his retirement David began doodling, as he calls it, for fun and a creative outlet. He is an avid giver and has donated time and beautiful images all over the city. David is involved with the Ronald McDonald house and refused to take payment for this book. A percentage will be donated in his honor.

Ms. Tina in the book is in honor and appreciation of the real Tina Lipari, LSCSW. Tina has shown more dedication and passion than any school social worker I have ever had the opportunity to collaborate with in my entire career. Tina values a collaborative approach and advocates and implements therapeutic outlets in every classroom. Her office is not just a school counselor's office, but a real place of hope and change. It is rare that children feel safe enough to dive into these issues at school, which speaks volumes about her ability to connect.

Corie English lives in Kansas City with her husband and two sons. She has been a photographer for twelve years and was inspired to take documentary style family photos during the pandemic to document the mood during the unprecedented time in history. Corie provided photos to assist with illustrations of the book and is a person who is moved by putting good out into the world.

When I feel my invisible riptide:
Who can I ask for help?

_____

_____

_____

_____

_____

_____

_____

_____

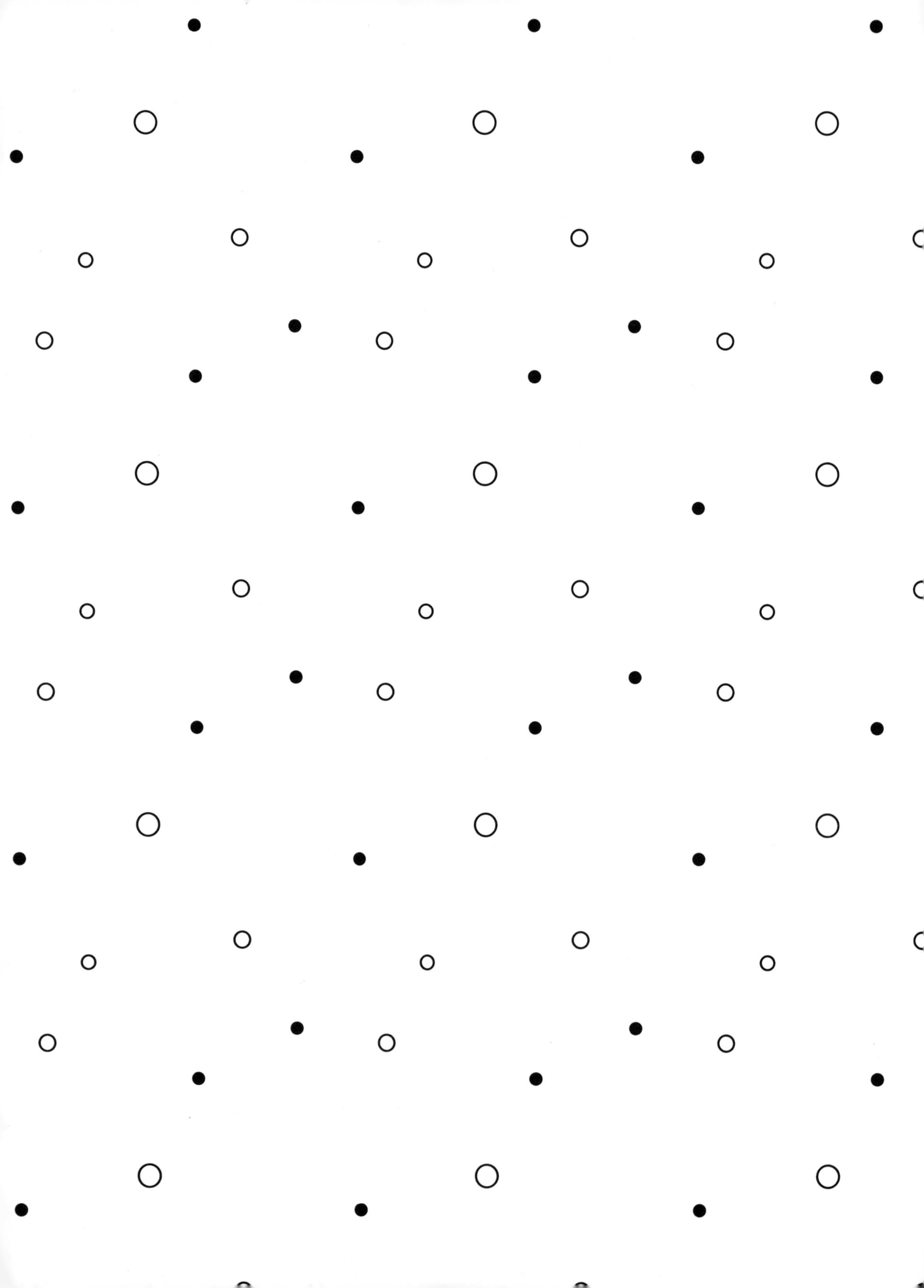